For my boys, Barry, Bill and Alfie, with love – SC

For Tiziana – JB-B

Created exclusively for World International Limited by Bloomsbury Publishing Plc
First published in Great Britain in 1997 by World International Limited, Deanway Technology Centre, Wilmslow Road, Handforth, Cheshire SK9 3FB

The moral right of the author and illustrator has been asserted
A CIP catalogue record of this book is available from the British Library

ISBN 0 7498 3087 5

Printed by Bath Press, Great Britain

10 9 8 7 6 5 4 3 2 1

Little Readers

The Silly Sisters

Susan Cunningham

Pictures by John Bendall-Brunello

World International Limited

Hello!
We're the
silly sisters.

I'm silly.
She's silly, and
she's silly too!

Don't be silly,
there are
only two
of us,
silly.

I'm LILLY, the silliest sister.
Dad says I'm a **silly sausage**.
But I say,

"What's so silly about SAUSAGES?"

Well, one day I found out.

I was sitting having tea, my favourite,
sausages and chips, when
the silly sausage
flipped!

Just like
that, off
my
plate,
over
the
ketchup
bottle,
and into
the cat's
dinner.

"Silly old
sausage," I said.
Well, that proves it.
"Pass the ketchup, sis."

And I'm **Tilly**, the other silly sister. When I'm really silly, **Lilly** calls me a **Silly Billy**. But I don't know why. Our friend **Billy** isn't silly at all.

Anyway, we think being silly is just about the best thing to be. Come on, **Lilly**, let's go and be silly!

Where shall we start?
I know! **Silly string!**

Spray it on the
cat's **whiskers,**

tie Dad's **shoelaces**
up in knots,

pop a little in
the pasta, give it a
stir - yum! yum!

give Granny a new **hairdo** — oops!
steady on the fringe, you'll
wake her up!

Right, all quiet again.
What's next?
I know! Let's be silly with Milly
next door! She loves it
when we're silly!

Give her a
clown's nose
and donkey's ears,

dress her up in Mum's
bikini and Dad's
groovy sunglasses,

plonk her there in the
pram until . . .

Quick! Scarper!
Here comes her dad!

OK, now what?
Silly faces!
You go first!

Raspberry face.

Pumpkin face.

Let's go upstairs. Hmm, feels a bit too sensible up here. **Come on!**

Time to be silly with Mum and Dad! Peep in! See if they're awake yet. They're not? **Great!**

Here we go! Paint Dad's toenails pink. Dab a bit of sun cream on his nose.

Powder Mum's hair - **whoops!**
It's gone all white!

And **now** for the **lipstick** . . .

Oh-oh! Mum's waking up.
Back to our rooms before
we get **rumbled** . . .

You're going to spend the day with Stanley.
He'll sort you out. " We look at each other. Stanley?
Sensible Stanley?

Spare us! Never mind,

we'll fix him with

our

maddest,

silliest

games.

At Stanley's house we
are silly with bells on.
Ready, steady, go!

Dip the
washing in the
dirty pond.

Dress the dog
in Stanley's
spotty pants.

Then Stanley looks at us and says in a sensible kind of voice:

"Don't be silly, you **silly sisters**.

I bet you won't be silly when Tom turns up."

"Don't be **silly**," we say, "of course we will."

And we carry on getting . . .

sillier
and
sillier
and
sillier.

Until
Tom
does
turn up . . .

Tom is so cool.

Tom is the best.

We want Tom to
be our friend.

So we try some of our favourite
silly things to impress
him. This is what we try.

We try double
treble wheelies
on our bikes.

We try our
back-to-front
hokey cokey dance.

We try out our newest, maddest jokes.

We even try our smelly fish face.

But Tom
  just looks at us
    and says in a deep,
      grown-up sort of voice,

"DON'T BE SILLY!"

We look at Tom.

We look at each other.

"Silly? US? Never!" we say.

Silly string
in the pasta?
Not us.

Dress Milly up
in donkey's ears?
Oh no.

Dip the
washing in
the dirty pond?
How vile.

Double treble
wheelies on our
bikes? **How silly!**

Smelly
fish
face?
Pooh,
pooh!

That's all
just SO - SILLY.

So
we're not
the silly sisters
any more. And now Tom
is our friend!

And when people
ask us our names,
we say,
"I'm Lilly and she's Tilly,
and . . .

we're . . .
just . . .
sisters!"

SILLY!